LITTLE RAINMAN

By: Karen L. Simmons

FUTURE HORIZONS INC.

LITTLE RAINMAN

All marketing and publishing rights guaranteed to and r̶e̶s̶e̶r̶v̶o̶y

FUTURE HORIZONS INC.

721 W. Abram Street
Arlington, TX 76013

800-489-0727

817-277-0727

817-277-2270 Fax

Website: www.FHautism.com
E-mail: info@FHautism.com

ISBN 10: 1-885477-29-5

ISBN 13: 978-1-885477-29-3

Preface

After my near death experience in 1994, I felt divinely inspired to write a book. At the time, I thought it was to be about the experience itself. I tried and nothing came. Not until I attended an autism conference in August of 1995 did I get chills and goose bumps thinking about this book, and the words just flowed through me. I like to say "this book was written through me" rather than "I wrote this book."

The incidence of autism or pervasive developmental disorder is on the rise in the world today. It is not solely due to an increase in occurrence, but is being recognized more at an earlier age and in milder forms. Also, the diagnostic criteria has changed, which alters the prevalence. What was once thought to be a disorder caused by parents is now known to be an actual neurobiological disorder that occurs before the child is born. In Massachusetts alone, the diagnosis of autism has increased by 500% in the last eight years according to Kathleen Quill, author of *Teaching Children with Autism: Strategies to Enhance Communication and Socialization.* She is an Associate Professor at Lesley College, Manchester, Massachusetts.

The reason I am writing this book is to help autistic children along with their parents, teachers, and siblings to understand as early as possible the real "world of autism." This will enable these children to get into an early intervention program as soon as possible. By doing so, they could have a very good prognosis as many children have had in recent years. My first thought was to write an operator's manual/handbook for my son's teachers or anyone involved in his life. This way they could more effectively know how to deal with his odd behavior in school or elsewhere. I could then simply hand out the book and say, "This is Jonathan. Please read about him, as he is different than most people." With each new year, there will be another series of classes in which I have to educate the new people involved in his life about who Jonathan really is. During an advanced conference on autism at The Geneva Centre in Toronto, Ontario, it was noted that autistic people learn better through written scripts if they are verbal and through pictures if they are nonverbal. This led me to the idea of writing his story. Since my son reads, I felt this would be the best way for him to understand himself and his condition of autism. Through the process of reading the actual script in his earlier years, he will understand how he is different from others and how others perceive him. My hope is that the world will learn to *enable* rather than *disable* autistic individuals in their lives.

This book is written *directly* by Karen Simmons and *indirectly* by my five year old son, Jonathan. I felt like I was literally inside of his head and writing what he truly feels. Autism occurs in many different degrees. My son happens to be a high-functioning autistic individual who is able to express himself at an early age. Unlike a lot of the autistic population, in which 50% are nonverbal and some have severe behavioral challenges such as head banging, he is able to function more effectively. He is like a window into the mind of a young autistic child. Though the book is directed to autistic people, it can also help teachers, parents, siblings and anyone else to recognize symptoms of autism at an early age. My hope is that this in turn can help to direct a lot more children into early intervention programs, giving them a much better chance in life.

My son is currently enrolled in an early intervention program and has been since the age of three and a half. We are doing all that we can in many avenues of treatment that we feel are appropriate for him. We also keep our minds open to new ideas and stay with what is working. I believe that getting him started in an early intervention program is the key to his progress.

In writing this I have worked through a lot of my own denial of my son's condition which would have only *slowed down* and interfered with his progress. I feel that each person in the world has been placed here for a reason, exactly the way they are, and all of these individuals are incredibly special. Each one of these precious autistic people need help learning in their own unique style in order for them to reach their own fullest potential. To act as facilitators in this process, I believe, is our role as family and educators. I was inspired to write this book by one twelve year old autistic boy in Toronto. He said, *"I never knew I had autism until I was nine. It would have helped me to understand who I was and how I was different if I would have known sooner. I would have a better quality of life, much happier and easier if I had known."*

The story as written are the actual events in my son's life. His thoughts and feelings are recorded as he has told me, both verbally and through his nonverbal actions. I have put his actual words in italics. I know this is how he felt at the time as any mother knows her own child. Many incidents have occurred, too numerous to mention, to lead me to this conclusion. This is actually how he worded his sentences at the time and is improving daily. Some dialogue, such as "my mom tells me" or "I have heard" I have added to help him and other autistic individuals understand autism better by reading the actual text.

I also wrote this as an actual script so he would learn by reading how he is different from others. I have added many pictures to help those unable to read also understand. Jonathan has read *Little Rainman* several times and I wasn't sure if he understood it or not. Six months after reading it, out of the blue he said *"Remember that book you wrote about me, Little Rainman, that was really cool how I flushed things down to Hoagie. I loved that book."* At other times since then, I have asked him about much of the content of the book. He remembers much of it and agrees with it. He can even laugh about what he used to do. Since he understands what would happen if he flew out of the window, he says *"I used to think I could fly"* or *"sometimes loud noises bother me but not always."* At least he knows he has autism and it's a good starting place for his life. He said he wanted to have a picture of us (Jonathan and myself) waving bye-bye at the end of this book. What it *means* to have autism is another story, which he said he would help me write about in another book.

Acknowledgments

First and foremost, I am grateful to all of my family for supporting the completion of this book. Without the patience, understanding and sixth sense ability of my children Kimberly, Matthew, Christina, Jonathan, Stephen and Alexander, I don't know how I could have finished. My husband Jim, was very understanding and tolerant, especially since I stayed up many nights until 2:00 a.m. I especially appreciate my mother, Mitzi Briehn, who has believed in me, and has shown me love and acceptance when I have doubted myself the most. My step-father Edward Briehn (Bunny) has been a great role model by always wearing a smile regardless of circumstances. My sister, Susan Simmons, was very supportive and encouraging during this process. My grandmother, Mama Nesse, has always been part of me and guided me down our spiritual path. My father, John Simmons, along with his love, has given me a sense of humor; and his late wife, Martha, has taught me that I can achieve my goals through my determination. My sister in-law, Anna, first brought Jonathan's differences to my attention when I didn't see them. My in-laws Joe, Josephine and Brian supported me in my endeavors.

I am very appreciative of the efforts of my publisher, Wayne Gilpin, of Future Horizons in Arlington, Texas. He and his staff have brought my vision to life without changing the manuscript.

I want to thank Gail Gillingham for proofreading my manuscript and giving me very good suggestions. I am grateful to Donna Williams for her correspondence and inspiration as well as Temple Grandin who will be using some of these illustrations in her presentations. Neil Walker and Ken Salzman from The Geneva Centre for Autism in Toronto, were also very helpful.

Rob Woodbury, the artist with autism, created the concepts for the illustrations from his perspective. Caraly Peterson, my son's aide, has been extremely helpful in her observations of Jonathan, as well as the expertise she has through working with other autistic individuals. Nancy Power, a wonderful friend, helped me get started in the publishing process. A very dear friend, Cyndi Harvey, whose life has paralleled mine for the past eight years, has helped me to believe in myself. Dr. Gerald Jampolsky, assisted me with names of publishers. Dr. Carol Ann Hapchin, Jonathan's Psychiatrist, also proofread the manuscript several times from her perspective.

Other special friends I would like to acknowledge are: Nancy and Dave Siever, Karen Knight, Dr. Dorothea Jones, Bill and Monica Bergman, Dr. Kan Lee, The Karpoffs, The Rowswelis, Cheryl Guyon, Frances South, Corinne Callan, Gwen Randall Young, Bev Crook, Vaun Gramatovich, Trish Hagen, Paula Coombs, Dr. and Mrs. Visconti, Dr. Goulden, Adele Parker and Bob Wilson. Each one of these people supported me during this process throug friendship and professional expertise. Dr. Morcos, Dr. Chyczij, Dr. Chetner and many other doctors at the Miscericordia Hospital were instrumental in giving me back my life. Val MacMillan, Jonathan's teacher, Susan Sieben, Resource Assistant, Margaret Galipeau, Physiotherapist, Audrey Cheney, Speech Therapist, and Sandra Moore, Teachers Assistant have all worked together within my son's Early Intervention Program. This took place within the Brentwood School in collaboration with the Robin Hood Association. John Convey, Principal, Bea Gursky, Special Needs Facilitator and all the teachers at Father Kenneth Kearns School have been very supportive through their belief in inclusion. Additionally, I wish to acknowledge the Four Mark's, a support group of teachers I have come to know. Also, Willson and Mary Anne Green for their assistance in selecting artwork.

I would especially like to acknowledge Enrico Bianco. He is a twelve year old boy with autism whom I met at the Geneva Centre Autism Conference in Toronto.   What he said was how he really wished he had known about his autism at an earlier age so he could have dealt with it more comfortably. Enrico was told about it but he didn't comprehend it until he was nine years old.

Many people, too numerous to mention, have been there for me before and during the publication of this book.   I wish to sincerely thank everyone I haven't mentioned who have assisted me in making *Little Rainman* possible.

Dedication

I dedicate this book first and foremost to my son, Jonathan. I love him dearly. In addition, it is sincerely dedicated to all of the children in the world with autism, that they may have a better life. The condition of autism can truly enrich the lives of the families as well as those involved with the individual.

This book is illustrated through the combined effort of three individuals: Rob Woodbury, a thirty year old high-functioning autistic individual who completed the original drawings; my mother, Mitzi Briehn; and my sister, Susan Simmons, who worked together to complete the drawings and enhance some of them with color.

My name is Jonathan. I have autism (aw-tis-um). My nose looks the same as other people's and my ears and eyes do too, except that I can see and hear a lot better than most people. My brain thinks different. Some things I do better, like reading and copying; other things I do worse, like making friends. I need help with learning to do some things. There aren't many people like me, maybe 15 in 10,000, so I am very unique. I will always need to learn how to cope in this world, which comes naturally to most other people.

When I was a baby I did not like to be touched or held, even by my parents. I would cry when I was picked up. My grandparents thought this was a bit odd, but everyone else didn't think much of it.

Back then when I was between one and two years old, I was fascinated with circles, and spinning my body around. I liked to spin things around and around, really fast. My parents had to re-connect the chandelier three times because I literally spinned it out of the ceiling. Also I would climb into the dishwasher and spin the bottom of it. Mom and I would play an exercise game. She would extend one leg in the air and say, "Circles in the air, circles in the air, switch," over and over again. I loved this game and would laugh very loud. I would always put the same leg in the air, though, not switching to the other. We don't play this anymore cause Mom says I get too attached to the game.

3

I like to spin around in circles. Mom says a lot of people with autism (like me) like to spin. We like wheels on cars, walking in circles, flapping our hands in the air, or even rocking back and forth. I also like to sing loud saying wee-wee-wee. It just makes me feel good to do this. They call it "stimming." All I know is that it makes me feel good even though Mom says most people think it is strange.

When I was younger, I didn't like to be touched because my skin was so sensitive. It would almost hurt to be touched, especially when I wasn't initiating the touching. People thought I only wanted to be alone. I couldn't stand crowds and didn't like to be with people. Of course I like people, it's just that I don't show it the same way most people do. I like to stay with people a lot more nowadays. I can stay in a room full of people for up to fifteen minutes! When I stay around people I sometimes stay safe inside my own head. It's like I have my safe space just for me. Most people have a two foot space around themselves when they don't want people to be too close to them; well, my space is about ten feet minimum! Being in crowds is still my least favorite thing to do.

7

I have a hard time thinking about more than one thing at a time. That's probably why I don't like to look into people's eyes when they are speaking to me. I just don't see any reason to look at them when they are talking. It seems uncomfortable for me to do this. This continues into my older years, even to this day. I'm almost five years old now. It's like I would rather hear what their eyes are telling me. I sort of look at them out of the corner of my eyes. Even though my vision is 20/20 I think something might be wrong with my eyes because I have a hard time catching a ball, and I accidentally bump into people lots of times. They get upset with me and sometimes cry. All I can say is "sorry." Mom is going to have my eyes checked out by a special eye doctor.

My favorite color used to be orange. Now it is blue. I really don't like red or yellow or black. Mostly I like light blue and dark blue and green. I have a new friend now named Cody. He is autistic too. We really liked each other a lot. It was like we were on the same wavelength. He thought a lot like me and it was hard for him to leave my house. I keep thinking of that guy. His mom says that he doesn't like bright colors at all. But he does like blue, gray and darker colors just like me.

I sometimes don't understand what people mean by the expression on their faces because I don't know what it means. Maybe someone is angry with me or doesn't want to play with me but I can't tell. Older people seem to think I should automatically know if someone doesn't want to play with me. I don't get it until it is too late.

Sounds are another thing. I can hear helicopters in the air before my brothers and sisters do. I say, "what's the noise?" When there are a lot of people in a room making a lot of racket, I sometimes have to leave the room. Also, I can't stand it when the blender is on. I say there is too much noise.

Mom told me that sounds from bright light bulbs really bother some autistic people. The humming drives them crazy. They just can't stand staying and listening to that loud buzzing sound. At night, the air conditioner vent in my room keeps me awake until very late. It bugs me a lot so I know how they feel.

17

Most recently, my mom had to take me out of tap dancing class. I kept mixing my feet up. When the class used their left foot to do their shuffle step, I used my right foot. It was so confusing, and the music and tapping were way too loud! I had to cover my ears with my hands to stand it. When we were marching, I slipped on my taps and fell. That's when I started crying from the inside of my heart. I was embarrassed and didn't want my tears to show so I kept them inside of me. Mom took me out and we didn't go back inside. She took me out for good.

Right afterwards, outside of the classroom, I saw a little girl. I wanted to see if anything was written on the back of her shirt like my shirt was. She wouldn't let me take off her sweater. Mom told me not to take someone else's clothes off that I don't even know. I still don't understand. I was trying to get to know her and to see her back. I also like to kiss people that I like. They will back away from me like I am sick or something. I guess I shouldn't do that.

Getting to know people is kind of like automatic glass doors. When you run up too fast, they don't open up. I think this is true with kids and grown ups. I have to be very careful not to make people think I am weird.

Mom also signed me up for Tae Kwon Do. I loved it so much but Ma'am and Sir (the teachers) got upset with me. I couldn't hold still and kept spinning around in circles and humming. The other kids kept staring at me. I just had a stomach ache and had to go pee. I was upset with Ma'am too cause she didn't understand me. Anyways, I kept kicking everybody for fun, even my brothers and sisters. So, they told my mom to take me out and maybe I could try again next year when I am six. I'm sure sad about it.

Some smells really bug me, like a stinky bathroom or something. Of course that bugs mostly everybody but I really can't stand it. Perfume, gasoline and even some people stink so much I used to not be able to stay in the same room with them. Now that I am used to more smells, it is easier to be around it. Cody, my new friend, can't stand the smell of tomato sauce to this day and he is already eleven years old. He is so funny, he calls his mom Gail instead of Mom and so do his brother and sister.

25

Sometimes the wallpaper on the wall starts to come off. I just can't stand when it is like that, some on and some off. I have to peel it off. I just have to. One piece at a time until it's all gone. I like the way it feels, and it bugs me when it isn't all in place too. Also, it sounds really neat to rip it off. Dad is having a fit but I think it is cool. I guess he'll just paint the wall or something.

I like to say things over and over again, over and over again, over and over again. Then I start to laugh. If my brother says, "What do you think you're doin?" then I will say, "What do you think you're doin?" right back to him. Mom told me this is called eck-oh-lail-e-ah because it sounds like an echo. Because I am autistic, I like to copy people this way.

Another thing that bugs me are my clothes. If they are scratchy or uncomfortable, then all that I can think of is getting those clothes off! I would rather wear no clothes at all if it's not too cold out. Clothes can wreck my day at school if they are wrong. I feel all tied up in knots if I have the wrong clothes on. I have my favorite outfit to wear. I wear it in the daytime and to sleep in. It feels so soft and it doesn't have any hard things in it. I would wear it every day if it didn't need washing.

When I first learned to walk, my steps were out of balance. I also went down stairs one step at a time. I did this by putting my left foot on the step below me and bringing my right foot down beside my left foot on the same step. I still do this. I feel like I might lose my balance going down the stairs, so I'd rather slide down the banister.

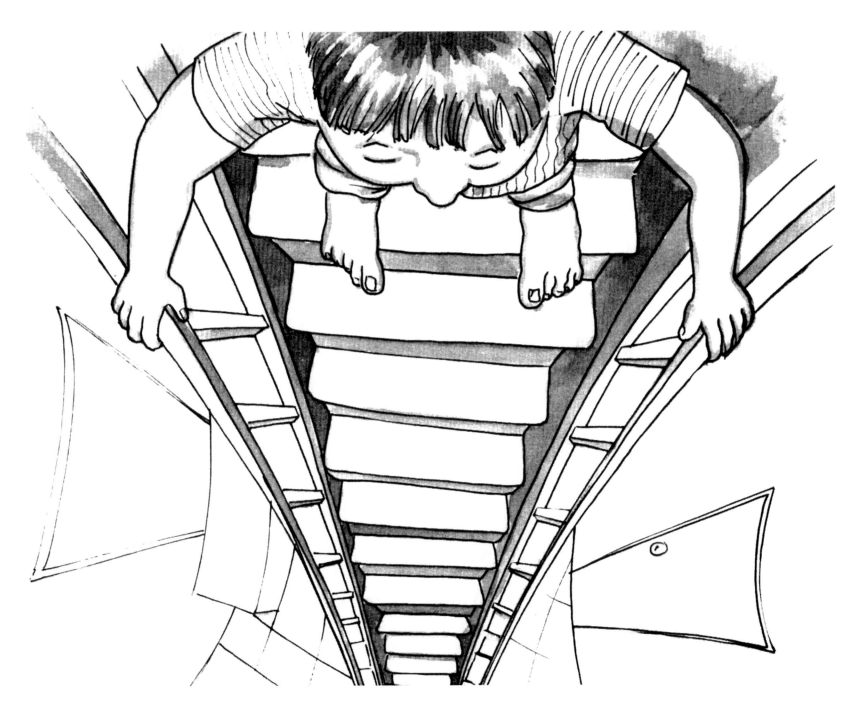

One time when I was just three I decided to go for a walk down the street. I had my diapers on and nothing else. There was snow on the ground and it felt good so I kept going, all the way to the big road. Some lady picked me up in her car and drove me around the neighborhood. The car stopped near my house and Mom came running to see if it was me in the car. The lady seemed very mad at Mom and Mom was very mad at me. I guess I should have told her I was going.

I love music and can remember a song backwards and forwards. An example: "I think you're A-one, grade A, beloved and beautiful, capable, caring, delightful, dependable, etc." but then I got sick of it and said, "No, no, no, no, stop stop stop." The tune goes around in my head for hours. My music teacher tells my mom

I can hit perfect notes and have great rhythm. Sometimes I forget where I am and continue to hum a tune even when a lot of people are around. People think this is a bit strange. I think it's okay though.

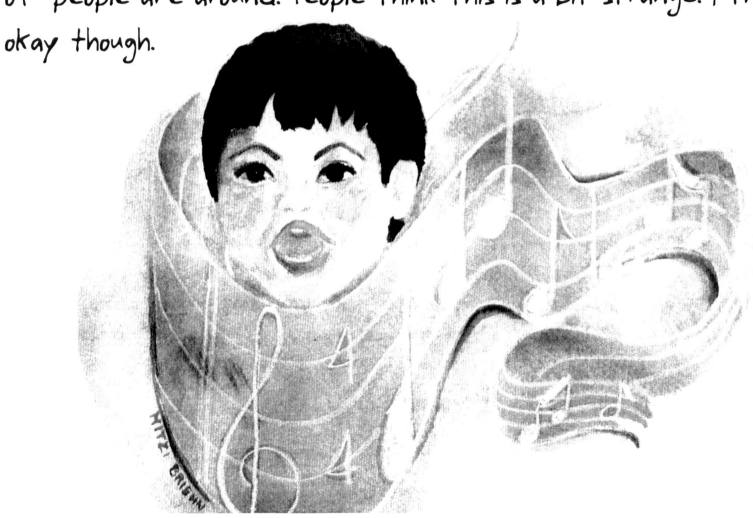

I began reading (out loud) when I was two and a half. Mom thinks I actually was reading sooner. My first word was "recycle." My parents and I were at the park when we walked by this truck that said recycle. I said ru-si-kul. They looked at each other in disbelief! In time words kept coming. I read everywhere I go, even the writing on bathroom walls. I went to a party and all I could say were the letters E - X - I - T out the door over and over and continued to go out the door around the side and back into the room. It was the only way I could stand being around all those people. I did this all night at that party. My parents didn't know what to do with me.

I get very upset with people when they don't understand me. I say, "You're not listening," or, "You got it all wrong, that's the wrong answer." Mom can tell in my voice I am upset. At least I can tell someone what is bothering me. I might get mad and push someone away or not talk to them, or cry. That doesn't mean I don't like them though. Mom says that some autistic people don't talk or read and the only way they talk to others is by pointing to pictures. I am sure glad I can talk. If I didn't, maybe I might get too upset and frustrated. I already get frustrated and kick sometimes so if I couldn't talk or read, it would be worse.

37

Every night I read myself to sleep with books that my ten-year-old sister lets me keep. Mom says that some kids with autism don't read and some don't talk. Mom thinks they must understand anyway, they just think different than most other people. So do I!

I like to read books about the body to help me go to sleep. One day my brother Matt was complaining about having a stomach ache. He said he didn't know why he had it. I said, "I get it, the food get carried to other parts of your body and that gives you a stomach ache." I think he knows now.

I like to know what is going to happen ahead of time or I get upset. That's one reason I like to watch movies over and over again. If I know what is going to happen, I'm happy, but if I am not sure what to expect then somebody like Caraly (my grown up helper) tells me I do some bizarre things, like throwing tantrums and dropping on the ground. She tells me not to do that anymore. I also may make noises or say something I heard in a movie once.

"Wheel of Fortune" and "Jeopardy" used to be my two favorite shows. I would stay glued to them for the entire show and want to watch it again. Now that I'm almost five, I like cartoons and other kid movies. I like to watch them over and over again, maybe fifty times. This way, I can memorize all the words and music. It makes me feel good to know the beginning and the end of each tape and also to know what comes next. Movies I can predict; people, I cannot.

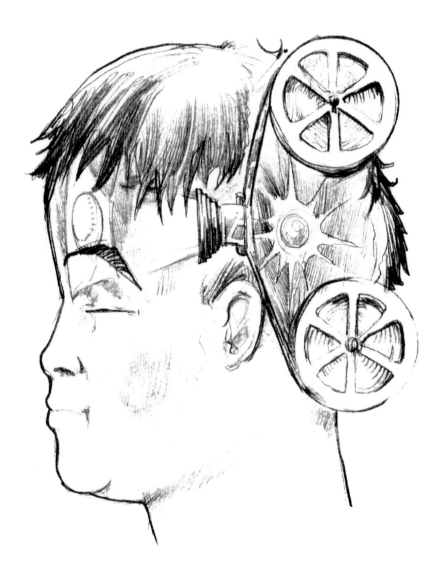

I like food but some foods I wouldn't even like to touch. Especially if it's all mixed together. I don't know what is in that stuff. It just looks too mixed up for me. Foods that I can pick up are usually good because they don't have sauce. Mushy food, like bananas, are yuck. Some drinks I don't like either. Mom says that a lot of autistic people are picky eaters. Of course, regular people can be too!

43

My computer is my favorite thing to play with. I think like it does and it thinks like I do. It makes me happy to be playing it, all the time if I could. We both think the same, exactly to the point. The computer's and my brain pick out just one piece of information at a time to focus on, not more. That's why the computer and I are so much alike. I can play on it for hours. In fact, I feel like I need to play on it sometimes just to calm down. I play Day of the Tentacle, Dr. Sebatio, and many other games and CDs. I can also get hung up on just entering and exiting the computer. This happened a lot when I first got interested in computers at the age of two.

In one computer game we flush things through the toilet to a guy named Hoagy. He is the fat guy in the program. Even when I wasn't playing with the computer, I used to say, "I'm Hoagy, the fat guy!" Mom says I get things that are not real mixed up with real things. I love to flush "things" to Hoagy. Mom has had to call the plumber many times.

One time I really scared my mom when I was Sonic the Hedgehog. I stood on her balcony and said, "Sonic wants to fly!" She thought I was going to jump. At the time I thought it would be fun cause I saw it on TV. After, Mom told me I could get killed if I jumped. I understand now. Instead I like to try and go down the laundry shoot. Mom doesn't let me do that either though. She says I would get stuck then she would have to call 911. I try when she is not around.

I enjoy doing things that I like to do, like reading and computing. Some things are easy for me to do like counting up to 200, playing computers, video games, reading and music. I also want to be liked and have friends. Friendships are hard for me. Just getting along with kids is very difficult.

When I play with someone, I can't talk to the kid and play at the same time. I like to do one or the other. Sometimes they just go away.

Sometimes people look at me strange when I say, "Hi I'm Richie Rich, the richest kid in the world." It is fun for me to pretend in this way. I like to be "Richie" until I find another character in a movie or in a computer game that I can become, just like the other night when we went to see Murmel Murmel Mortimer Munch. Then I was Mortimer and Mom was Mortimer's Mom. Lately I haven't wanted to be anyone at all except me. For Halloween I am going to be a plain boy!

My feelings get hurt very easy and sometimes I cry and tell someone that I am very sad. Sometimes I believe people too much. They tell me something I believe and they trick me. I like kids to like me and I like some kids too, but some are very mean. I know I'm different and I just want to know how and fit in. I might do a lot to get someone to like me, sometimes to the point of being stupid. Mom told me about a boy that was sixteen years old. He was autistic. Another guy told this boy to get on the floor and bark like a dog. The boy did because he thought he would be his friend then. A bunch of guys just laughed at him and hurt his feelings. His teacher told him to tell those boys to leave him alone. He didn't do anything silly like that again. Real friends wouldn't ask him to make a fool of himself. I hope I don't fall for something like that when I get older.

My grown up helper got hurt by an autistic teenager who hit her. He broke her hand. He was mad because he was hungry and he wanted food right then. I also like to do what I want to do when I want to do it. I feel this way but I'm learning to accept no for an answer sometimes. Grown-ups need to have a lot of patience with me. I can get lost without rigid rules. When I was younger, dinner had to be on the table exactly at 5:00 PM or my parents couldn't get me to the table without a fight.

I talk differently than other people. My mom tries to correct me when I say I don't want "no" mayonnaise, but I know differently. (At least my way seems right.) She will repeat it her way until I finally memorize her way but I still don't understand what makes her way right.

55

Also, some kids call me stupid and a retard because I talk slower than they do. I think it just takes me longer to think of an answer than other people. It is because I wasn't already thinking about it. I was probably thinking about something else. My brother must think my brain has a lot of compartments like boxes in it. It's because I have to focus really hard on one thing at a time, since so many other things are happening at the same time. He thinks I can't hear him when I really can. It's just that I am working on something else. I try to picture exactly what people are saying. When someone says, "It's raining cats and dogs," I look up to the sky to see if any animals are coming down.

A few months ago, we were playing a video game called "Lost Vikings." They played with knives inside the game so I wanted to do that also when I got home. I went upstairs to get the biggest one I could find, so I could kill the enemy. After all, isn't that what we're supposed to do, get rid of the bad guys?

Another time Mom was driving five of us kids back from computer class. I thought Tetris was a really cool computer game. Matt started to scream when I decided to play it on his head with a book. Mom said it seemed like a harmless game until that happened.

Sometimes I get upset from all the stuff going on. Everything is coming at me from all directions, and I feel like running away. Sometimes I do and I forget to tell anyone. One time I decided to bring my little brother, Stephen, to climb a chimney at someone else's house. Mom caught us and got really mad at me.

If I don't want to go someplace I say, "School is closed, I think it is all locked up." My way of saying this is different than my brother's. He would say, "I don't want to go to school!"

I'm glad I have my sisters and brothers. It forces me to get along with kids even when I don't want to. They teach me a lot and we love each other. They tell their friends how I am different and unique. I even went to my brother's grade three class and read a book in front of the class. Matt, Kim and Christina were so proud of me. Some kids understand about me and some don't. I like to fit in and play but some kids are nice to me and others aren't.

63

I'm just like everybody. I want friends and want to be liked too. I want to be loved and accepted for who I am and never be made fun of. I like to fit in. Mom tells me I am different and special. She also says I am very smart. I get the feeling that I truly am because of how I get treated by some people.

What I really want in life is to be happy, have lots of fun and for people to like me.

Jonathan S.

65